words and images by
Adela Turin and Nella Bosnia

*the real story
of the bonobos
who wore spectacles*

non-sexist children's literature

Writers and Readers Publishing Cooperative

A very very long time ago, the bonobos
lived in a mangrove glade.
They spent their time munching the fruit
and berries, nuts and seeds, roots and buds,
which the women, the bonobesses,
gathered for them and for the bonobabies.

The bonobos, perched atop the mangrove trees, munched and munched, chattered, clapped their hands and beat away on the tree trunks. All this created a din which could be heard for miles about. The neighbouring pongolins and slothkins, who as everyone knows enjoy a midday snooze, used to complain bitterly.

One fine day, the bonobos got tired
of constantly repeating the same stories
and they decided to educate themselves.
After days and weeks of discussions, debates,
elections, conclusions and decisions...

...*the four finest bonobos
set out for Bordeaux to study French.*

Those who stayed behind continued
to chatter and clap and munch the fruit
and berries, nuts and seeds, roots and buds
which the bonobesses continued
conscientiously to gather for them. Then
one fine Tuesday, the four fine bonobos
returned from Bordeaux. Everyone
could see that each one was wearing
spectacles and carrying a black suitcase.

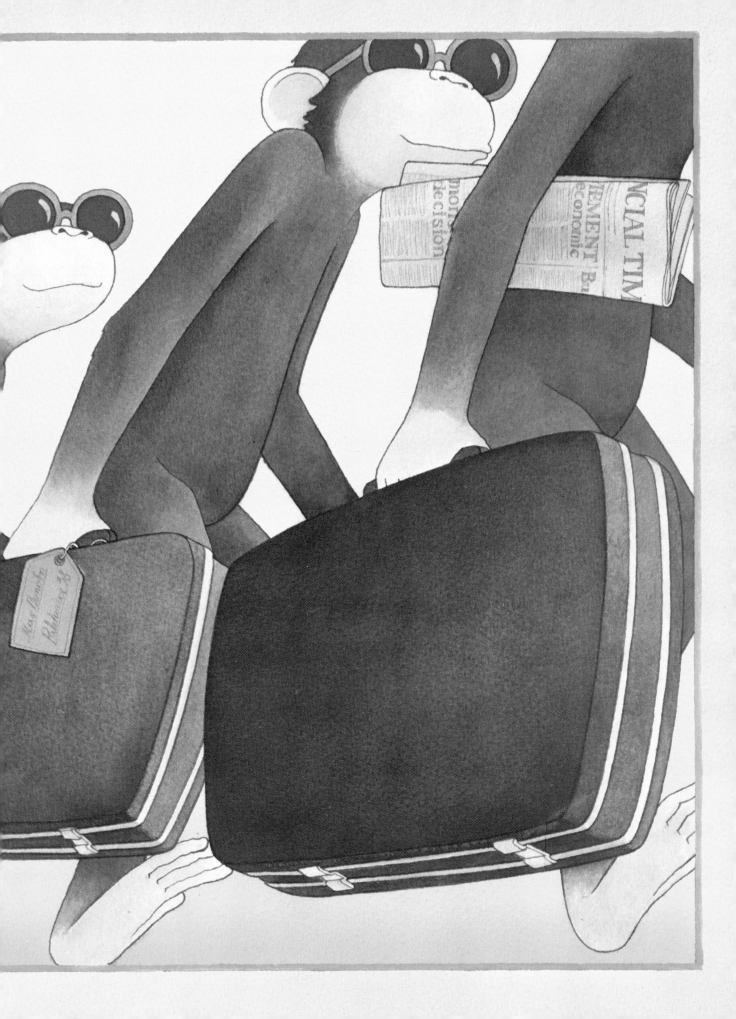

The four bespectacled bonobos settled
themselves on top of the tallest tree and
for a whole day, they shouted strange
words which noone had ever heard
or could understand: "Mer! Nuit! Noir! Air!"
Naturally all the other bonobos
were filled with admiration.

And so the bespectacled bonobos
began to teach the others the words.
The bonobesses brought them double rations
of fruits and berries, nuts and seeds,
roots and buds, while the other bonobos
learnt the strange new words.
Come examination time, any bonobo
who had mastered the four words
received a fine pair of spectacles which were
solemnly taken out
of the black suitcases. After a while,
all the bonobos knew the words
and all wore spectacles.

Of course, the bonobesses who had listened to the lessons knew the words too. But they were not given any spectacles. It was the custom for bonobesses to wear headscarves, and spectacles just would not stay put. A few bonobesses tried to get rid of their headscarves so as to be able to wear spectacles. But the bonobos laughed so sarcastically

t this sight, that the few brave bonobesses hurried
o put their scarves back on again.
It's just as well," thought the bonobos. "If the bonobesses
tarted teaching too, then who would gather
he fruit and berries, nuts and seeds, roots and buds
or us and the bonobabies?"

But the bonobesses
had had quite enough of gathering
so much fruit and so many berries, nuts and
seeds and buds, and of listening
to the same words, which after a while
had begun to get on their nerves.
So one day, they decided to move to another
mangrove glade and they resolved to do
only what they felt like doing.

One bonobess planted flowers around the trees. Another created a herb garden which perfumed the whole glade. Another whittled a willow twig into a flute and started playing such lovely music that the pongolins and slothkins quite forgot to take their midday snooze, a rare thing indeed.

Still other bonobesses constructed kites for windy days, and hammocks for hot summer nights.

Other bonobesses made blankets for cold nights, folding umbrellas for rainy days, toys for the bonobabies and musical instruments which became more and more intricate and melodious. The mangrove glade grew beautiful and comfortable. The air was full of laughter and music and the scent of flowers. The bonobesses and bonobabies gathered nuts and buds and roots and seeds which they all shared together.

And so the bonobos, driven by hunger, were forced to come down from the trees to look for their own food. Since they were not used to this, they had difficulty at first in finding the fruits and berries, nuts and seeds. Taking off their spectacles in order to see better, they spent whole days silently searching the undergrowth for food.

The four strange words were forgotten;
the rain fell and the grass grew over
the black suitcases and broken spectacles.

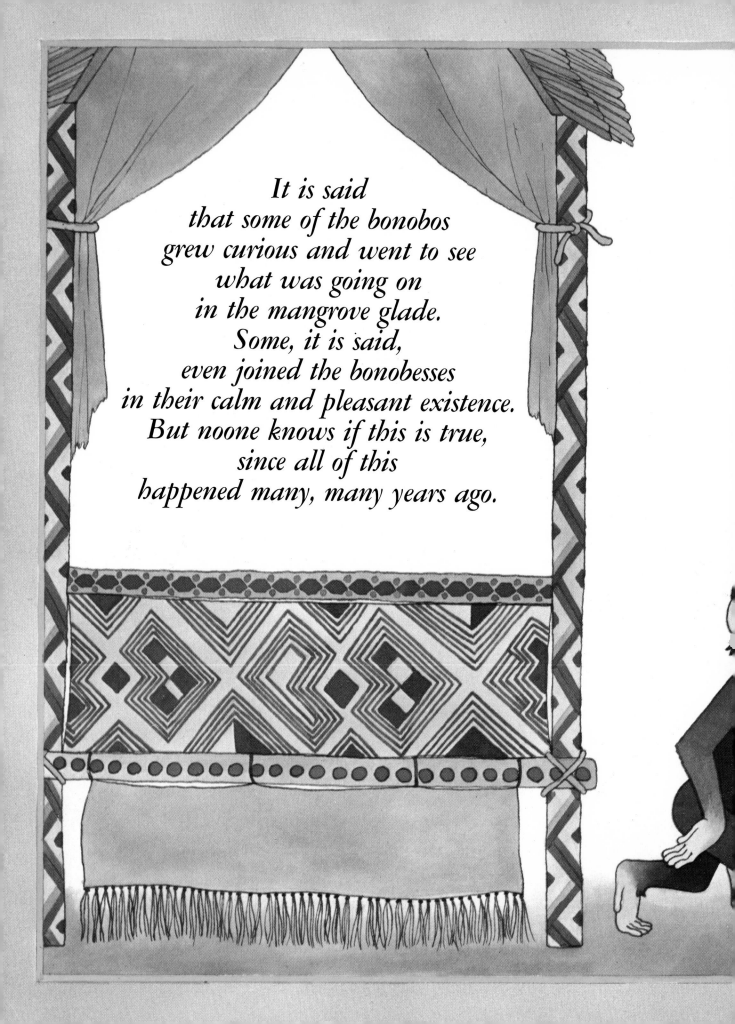

It is said
that some of the bonobos
grew curious and went to see
what was going on
in the mangrove glade.
Some, it is said,
even joined the bonobesses
in their calm and pleasant existence.
But noone knows if this is true,
since all of this
happened many, many years ago.